The Truck That Drove All Night

by Lynn Offerman / illustrated by Patti Boy

A GOLDEN BOOK • NEW YORK
Western Publishing Company, Inc., Racine, Wisconsin 53404

In the little town
the sun goes down.

Bunnies are sleeping.
Babies are sleeping.

But someone is awake.

Behind the blue gate,
a light is on.

Charlie, the truck driver,
eats coffee and cake.

He makes up his bed
and hugs his pal, Ted.

Then he turns out the light
and goes into the night.

Outside the blue gate
a yellow truck waits.
It's Old Roller Mack,
Charlie's hauler
and friend.

The moon comes up.
Charlie climbs in.

He turns the key,
pushes the pedal,
starts the engine,
tests the brake.

The headlights are on.
The taillights are on.
Ready, set, go!

Mack goes up a big hill
under the stars,
and down another one
lit by cars.

Later, the moon is hidden.
Splat! What's that? Rain.

Clang! Clang! Hoot!
Here comes a train.

OLeman River 3 miles

Thunder claps crack overhead.
Old Mack's taillights flash bright red.

Houses, headlights, and trees rush past.
Then old Mack comes to the river at last.

At the quiet dock,
the sun comes up.
Big steamer, wake up.
Little tugboat, wake up.

But someone is sleeping.

Next to the river,
where the waves hit the shores,
Charlie eats breakfast.

And Old Mack just snores.